Stella gasped. "Can I really?"
"I was joking!" laughed Mum.
But Stella wasn't.

Next day, Stella told Mum she
was definitely going to Space School.
"There's one right here in the forest!" she said.

Mum worried it would be scary out in space,
but Stella wasn't frightened . . . until she
spotted the queue outside the school.
"What if I don't get in?" she said.
"You will!" said Mum. "Squirrels
can do anything!"

# ANIMAL EXPLORERS

## STELLA THE ASTRONAUT

ALISON GREEN BOOKS

It was bedtime, but
Stella was gazing at the stars.
"Can squirrels fly to the moon?"
she asked her mum.

"You'd have to go to Space School,"
said Mum, "and train to be
an astronaut."

So Stella joined the queue. Everyone else was a lot taller, but Stella was the most determined.

You have to pass lots of tests to go to Space School. Stella was doing really well . . .

A really difficult maths problem

54 moon rocks x 3 = 162
25 stars + 36 stars = 61
600 comets ÷ 50 = 12
235
rocks, stars and comets

Minimum height

. . . until it came to the Height Test. Lionel, the instructor, measured her.

"Too short!" he said. "Next!" Stella was devastated – surely she couldn't give up yet?

As the lucky candidates started their Space School training, she decided to sneak in and listen.

The Solar System

She was so small, nobody noticed. It was amazing learning all about space and science!

After that, Stella slipped into every single class. But it wasn't always easy staying hidden.

She was ordered out of Space Walking class . . .

. . . and Moon-Buggy Driving class . . .

. . . and Zero Gravity class.
"Stella!" said Lionel, sternly.
"You will never be an astronaut.
You're too small!"

But Stella couldn't quite give up hope.

With training over, three top astronauts were chosen to fly to the moon. Stella was so sad not to be going with them. She decided to do some more weight training instead. (Astronauts have to be very fit and strong.) Maybe one day her turn would come. If only she could grow a bit taller!

Then, on Launch Day, Stella got a big surprise.

Everyone was ready for takeoff . . .
except for Koala. He'd put his spacesuit
in the wash, and it had shrunk.
He couldn't possibly wear it now.

"Mission cancelled!" groaned Lionel.
He was about to send everyone home,
when Stella cried . . .

"I'll go!"

"You?" growled Lionel.
"You're just a squirrel!"
"But I'm really strong," said Stella.
"I've done all the lessons.

"And Koala's
spacesuit is a perfect fit!"
Lionel sighed. "All right," he said.
"You can go. Just don't mess up!"

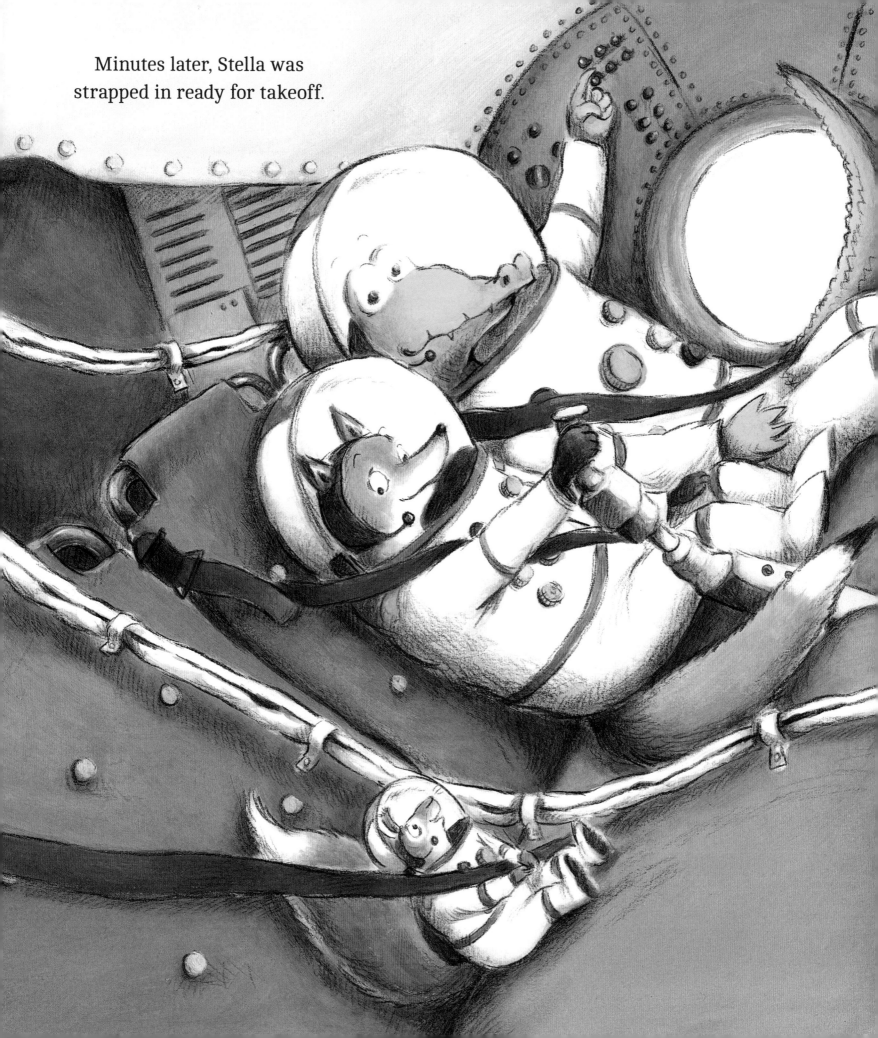

Minutes later, Stella was
strapped in ready for takeoff.

Her mum
watched proudly as
Lionel counted down.

5 – 4 – 3 – 2 – 1 . . .

# LIFT-OFF!!!

Stella was the first-ever squirrel in space!

With three days to fly to
the moon, there was time to relax.

It's not easy eating your dinner in zero
gravity. It was a bit of a squash, too.
"I'm glad you're so little, Stella!"
said Fox.

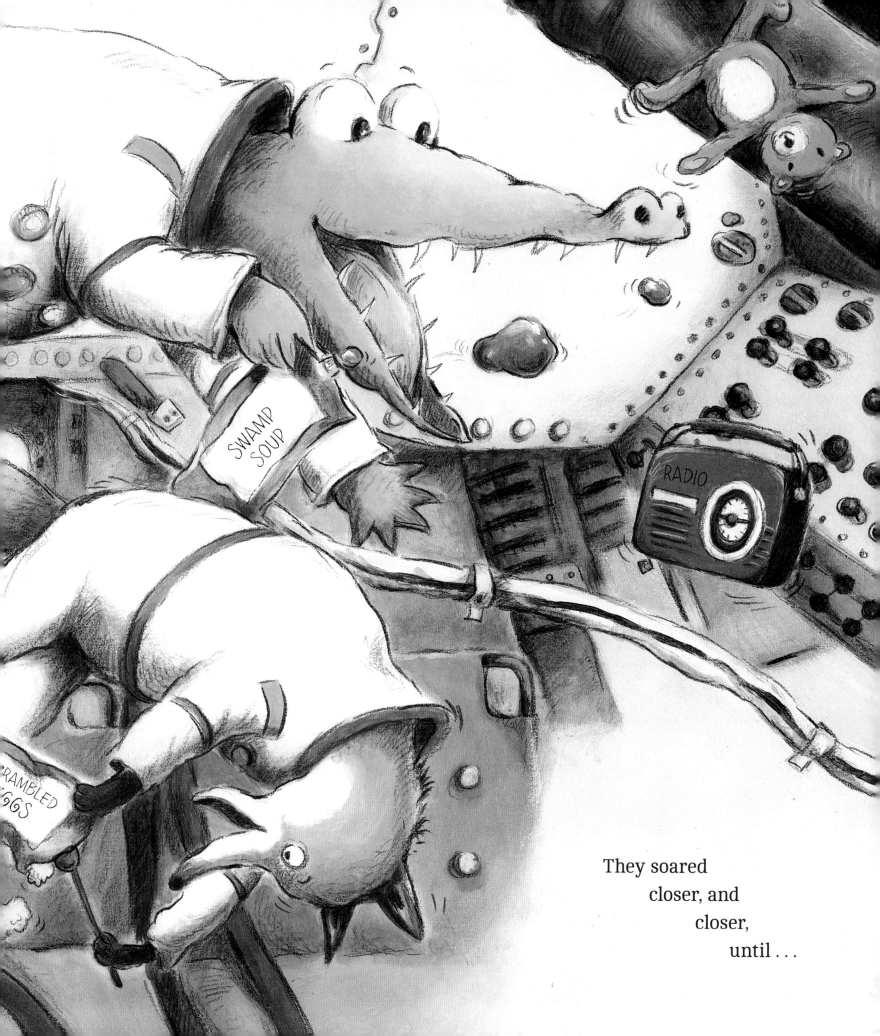

They soared
closer, and
closer,
until . . .

# There it was! The moon!

The astronauts were very
excite, but a bit nervous, too.

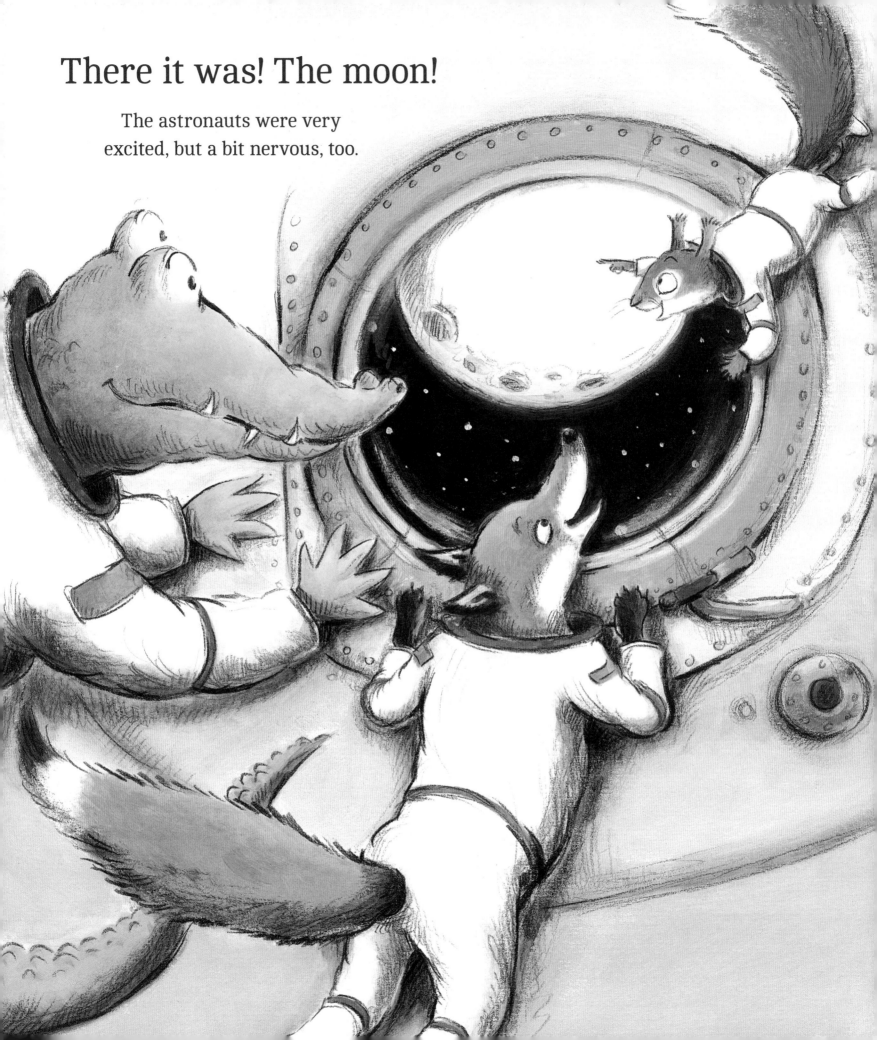

It was time to part company with Fox.
He'd stay in orbit, while Stella and Croc
landed the lunar module.

As they stepped outside, Stella
gazed back at Planet Earth. It was strange to
think that somewhere down there was her home.
"Come on, Stella," said Croc. "Let's go for a moon walk!"

Stella could have played in zero gravity all day long.

But there was too much work to do.

They had to take photos . . .

Huge craters!

Croc's footprint

Making moon-dust angels!

. . . and collect moon dust
and moon rocks.

Croc could lift the
biggest rocks . . .

... but Stella was best at driving the moon buggy.

They planted a flag and radioed Lionel at Mission Control.

"Congratulations, team!" said Lionel.
"I'm proud of you all. And well done, Stella.
You've shown what a squirrel can do!"

As they zoomed back to Earth,
Stella gazed out of the window.

There was so much space to explore.
She wondered where her next trip
would take her. Maybe Mars?

As Stella discovered, it's
not easy getting chosen for a
space mission. Just a few hundred
people have soared into space, and only
twelve have actually walked on the moon.
Could humans (or squirrels!) ever travel
to the planet Mars? Not quite yet . . .
but scientists are working hard
to make it possible.

# Stella's adventures are inspired by some famous real-life astronauts and scientists:

## YURI GAGARIN
### (1934-1968)

### FIRST HUMAN BEING IN SPACE

Despite a very hard childhood growing up on a farm, Yuri had an extraordinary life. He learned to fly planes, but soon set his sights higher. He was chosen from over 200 candidates to train as a cosmonaut (a Russian astronaut).

On April 12, 1961, Yuri blasted into space in the Vostok 1 spacecraft. He had to be strong, calm, confident, and incredibly brave. No one knew how the flight would go, or whether he'd even survive. Luckily, after orbiting the Earth for 108 minutes, Yuri returned unharmed. He was a hero all over the world, and an inspiration to astronauts everywhere.

## NEIL ARMSTRONG & BUZZ ALDRIN
### (1930-2012 & 1930- )

### FIRST TO WALK ON THE MOON

Like Yuri Gagarin, Armstrong and Aldrin trained as pilots before becoming astronauts. On July 16, 1969, they and fellow astronaut Michael Collins blasted off on the Apollo 11 space mission. It took four days to travel the 376,400 kilometres to the moon. While Collins orbited in the command module, Aldrin and Armstrong landed the lunar module – and stepped on to the moon!

They planted a flag, collected rock samples and set up scientific equipment. Aldrin even took the first selfie in space! Then they rejoined Collins and travelled back to Earth, splashing down in the Pacific Ocean. Their footprints remain on the moon to this day.

## KATHERINE JOHNSON
### (1918-2020)

### BRILLIANT MATHEMATICIAN

It takes an extraordinary team of people to launch a space mission, and Katherine was one of the most extraordinary of all. She had an amazing gift for maths, and was soon several grades ahead at school. After working as a teacher, she joined the American space agency, NASA.

Katherine had to fight hard against racial prejudice, but her determination paid off and she played a critical role in many space missions.

Without using a computer, she worked out the astronauts' flight paths, calculating when and where they'd land. Astronauts trusted that Katherine's super-accurate calculations would keep them safe – and they were right!

For Oliver and
Benjamin Gamazo

Published in the UK by Alison Green Books, 2022
An imprint of Scholastic
Euston House, 24 Eversholt Street, London NW1 1DB
Scholastic Ireland, 89E Lagan Road, Dublin Industrial Estate,
Glasnevin, Dublin D11 HP5F

www.scholastic.co.uk

Designed by Zoë Tucker

HB ISBN: 978 0 702307 61 4
PB ISBN: 978 0 702307 62 1